FR3VR

BY ANDY BELL

ILLUSTRATED BY

PETER HORNELAND

Published by Page 130 Productions

IN

ALL

LIFE

IS BIRTH

IS DEATH

IS REBIRTH

AND RE-DEATH

FIRST GASP

LAST BREATH

IN EARTH

INTERRED

FROM NOTHING
TO NOWT
WHAT IS LIFE ABOUT?

TO PROCESS
THE MATTER
'TIL NOTHING IS LEFT

FROM SOMETHING
TO SOMEONE
WHAT TIME IS DEATH?

FROM THE FRUIT OF LOINS
TO FEEDING THE TREE
IGNORE AT YOUR PERIL
LIFE'S CRUEL SYMMETRY

THE

SANDS

OF

TIME

1.

TO GO HOME TO A PLACE

YOU NO LONGER BELIEVE

YOU'RE GOING TO NEED

ALL TIME AND

ALL SPACE

2.

TO RETURN TO YOUR PLANET

WHERE ALL TIME HAS STOOD STILL

WILL REQUIRE ALL THE WILL

YOUR MIND

CAN MANAGE

3.

TO ESCAPE FROM THIS MAN

WHO EXISTS OUT OF TIME

WHO HAS DRAWN THIS LINE

IN APOPHENIAN SANDS

4.

HE SEEKS AN ENCOUNTER

BEHIND THE GREEN CURTAIN

FOR EVERY MEGATON

BURNED INTO

HIS SOUL

5.

HIS SOUL IS FORSAKEN

MORALITY LONG CEASED

FROM EVIL RELEASED

IN SHIMA

THAT DAY

6.

TO EXIST OUT OF TIME

SEE DECAY IN HIS FRIENDS

BEGINNING TO END

ALL PARTNERS

IN CRIME

7.

CURS-ED TO REMEMEMBER
FROM YOSHI TO THE CLARKS
THE VERY BRIGHTEST SPARKS
DEAR FLAME AND
EMBER

8.

HIS LOYAL COMPANIONS
FROM FOUNTAIN TO THE POOL
COLLECT GOLDEN APPLES
REBORN
MELANION

9.

RACING ATALANTA

ACROSS TIME AND SPACE

APHRODITE'S GRACE

RESONANT

MANTRA

10.

THE GIRL THAT REMEMBERED

ORIGINS OF US ALL

INSIDE PYRAMID TALL

WITH GLOWING

EMBERS

11.

THE PYRE IN THE MIDDLE
A FIRE BURNS AT ITS HEART
THE PLACE WHERE WE ALL START
TO LIVE LIFE'S
RIDDLE

12.

FOR WHAT HAS COME BEFORE
IS NOTHING BUT THE CODE
BUT THIS FUTURE'S OPEN ROAD
CAN BE READ
NO MORE

13.

OUR LUCY WAS THE GLITCH
HALTING REAL ELON'S PLAN
FREEZE THE SIMULATION
TASSO FLICKS
THE SWITCH

14.

DO OUR TWINS REUNITE?
ABOVE US, JET AND SKY
SPLIT, REALITY UNDONE
TOGETHER
RE-TIED

15.

THE DARKNESS OF WHAT'S GONE
THE DARKNESS OF WHAT'S LEFT
GRIEF LEAVES US ALL BEREFT
OF LIGHT FROM
THE SUN

16.

SO YOU TAKE THEM WITH YOU
FOR THE REST OF THE RIDE
KEEP THEM ON THE INSIDE
YOU BEGIN
ANEW

17.

FROM DEATH, THEY STAY TO SPEAK
AND WATCH AND LISTEN TO
AND CUT LIFE'S BUMPS IN TWO
BRING BEAUTY
TO BLEAK

18.

BRINGING MEANING TO LIFE
BY LIVING AFTER DEATH
REBIRTHING WHAT IS LEFT
OUR FUTURE'S
MIDWIFE

19.

CAPTAIN CLARK HAS HIS EVE

TOGETHER, SAFE ON TITAN

JOURNEY'S END, ENLIGHTENS

REALITY

PERCEIVED

20.

PADRE GONE TO MAGDALENE

TO CALVARY, RETURNED

AND NEW LESSONS UNLEARNED

MAJOR TOM

AGAIN

21.

AN ANCIENT ASTRONAUT

AND A PENITENT THIEF

HE CARRIES ALL OUR GRIEF

GIVES US FOOD

FOR THOUGHT

22.

LOST AT THE EDGE OF TIME

LUCY TAYLOR AND THIS MAN

WHO SEEKS TO UNDERSTAND

REALITY

SUBLIME

23.

MEANWHILE, IN THE CAGE
SHE COMES TO SAVE THE DAY
SHE HOPES TO FIND A WAY
TO TURN THE
NEXT PAGE

BLACK

OR

WHITE

I.

ALONG AN ENDLESS PLANE

GROW PYRAMIDS SO BRIGHT

COLOURED BLACK AND WHITE

DRAWS ALL TO

THE FLAME

2.

WHICH FIRE THEY MUST DECIDE

WHITE OR BLACK IGNITION

ONE GRANTS OUR SALVATION

THE OTHER

SUICIDE

3.

THE WHITE ROOM IS THE   PLACE
WHERE ALL STORIES ARE TOLD
MORE ANCIENT THAN THE OLD
JUSTIFIED
EMBRACE

4.

THE WHITE ROOM IS A PROMISE
ANSWERS TO ALL THAT ASK
WHO IS BEHIND THE MASK?
INITIATE
NOVICE

5.

THE WHITE ROOM LIGHT BLINDS US

FROM ALL THAT DOES US HARM

ALL RESIDENTS CONFORM

WATCHTOWERS WILL

GUIDE US

6.

THE WHITE ROOM GIVES US BLISS

OUR BODIES ATOMISED

BANISH COLLECTIVE SIGHS

TOGETHER

ONE VOICE

7.

THE WHITE ROOM KEEPS US SAFE

FROM NEGATIVITY

SUPPORTING CLIVITY

CUSHIONED FROM

THE QUAKE

8.

THE BLACK ROOM IS A CELL

WITHOUT WINDOWS AND DOORS

WITHOUT WALLS FOR EVERMORE

KALI FOR

HOTEL

9.

THE BLACK ROOM IS A SONG

CHANTED FOR MILLENIA

MANKIND'S SCHIZOPHRENIA

FREE LOVE OR

THE BOMB

10.

THE BLACK ROOM CALLS TO ARMS

ALL THOSE THAT WOULD REBEL

WITH STORIES STILL TO TELL

WITH ALL FEARS

DISARMED

11.

THE BLACK ROOM IS NOT DEATH

DESTRUCTION OR DECAY

WHERE CHAOS HAS ITS WAY

ON ALL

SHIBBOLETHS

12.

THE BLACK ROOM IS REBIRTH

A CHANCE TO SHED A SKIN

TO SHOW WHAT LIES WITHIN

SHACKLED

PLANET EARTH

13.

CHARLES AND LUCY TAYLOR

THE TIME THIEF AND THE GLITCH

APPROACH A DISTANT RIDGE

ABOVE A VAST CRATER

14.

WHAT STRUCK HERE IS LONG GONE

ALL THAT REMAINS IS VOID

FROM COSMIC SCHADENFREUDE

BLASTS TO MATCH

THE BOMB

15.

"DEAR LUCY. CAN YOU SEE?
WHAT OUR MAKER DID TO ME
CREATED DICHOTOMY
PRESERVED
ETERNITY"

16.

"WHO KNOWS WHERE THE TIME GOES?
WHEN ALL YOU HAVE IS NOW
WHEN ALL THAT HE ALLOWS
IS WHAT I
PROPOSE"

17.

"WE HAVE A CHOICE TO CHOOSE
TWO ROOMS OF BLACK AND WHITE
ONE EACH WE MUST DECIDE
TELL ME
WHO WILL LOSE?"

18.

"IT'S TIME TO PART OUR WAYS
OUR PATHS MUST NOW DIVERGE
ONE PYRAMID WILL PURGE
THE OTHER
DECIMATE"

19.

"OFF'RING NO CHIVALRY
I'M AFRAID MY CHOICE IS MADE
I CHOSE GLORIOUS WHITE
YOU CAN'T COME
WITH ME"

20.

"DEAR LUCY. GO TO BLACK
MY MAKER WAITS IN WHITE
FOR ME, UNTOLD DELIGHTS
THEN I WILL
GO BACK"

21.

"TO FROZEN EARTH, OUR HOME
I'LL BE PERCEIVED A GOD
DIVINE WHAT NUMBER'S ODD
LEAVE YOU ALL
ALONE"

22.

AND WITH THAT CHARLES DID GO
THROUGH THE WHITE ROOM'S DOOR
HE DID NOT SEE THE FLAW
IN ELON'S
MAGIC SHOW

23.

FOR TRICKSTER ELON BITES
NO WISH TO ANSWER BACK
FOR THE WHITE ROOM'S BLACK, AND
THE BLACK ROOM
IS WHITE

BLACK

TURNS

TO

GOLD

1.

AS LUCY ENTERED WHITE

CHARLES WAS ENGULFED BY BLACK

REALITIES DID CRACK

POTENTIALS

IGNITE

2.

IN PYRAMID OF WHITE

RESIDES A ROOM OF BLACK

DEVOID OF HABITAT

FEATURELESS

IN SIGHT

3.

IN PYRAMID OF BLACK

RESIDES A ROOM OF WHITE

BLINDED BY BRIGHT LIGHT

UNFORESEEN

CONTRACT

4.

CHARLES SCREAMING AT THE VOID

MANKIND VERSUS MAKER

NO ANSWER FROM CREATOR

FUTURE DREAMS

DESTROYED

5.

AND WHAT YOU ASK OF ELON?

HE MUTES CATASHI'S SCREAMS

JUST PIXELS ON A SCREEN

ONE LESS SOUL

TO RUN

6.

NO WINDOWS AND NO DOORS

TIME THIEF HELD ETERNAL

BLACK ROOM FIRES INFERNAL

WAR TO END

ALL WARS

7.

FLAMES RESURRECT OLD SCARS
TICK COMES AFTER THE TOCK
A LIFE BACK ON THE CLOCK
BURNING UP
LIKE STARS

8.

FATE HANDED HIM A CURSE
LIFE WITHOUT FEAR OF DEATH
BUT HE BREATHES HIS FINAL BREATH
FINALLY
RELEASED

9.

AND WHAT OF LUCY TAYLOR

ENCASED IN PUREST WHITE

TIME TO REIGNITE. WITH

TASSO

HER SAVIOUR

10.

BRILLIANT VOID REVEALS

THE COMING OF THE CAGE

FROM DAMANHUR IT CAME

TRAVELS

WITHOUT WHEELS

11.

GO TO THE END OF TIME
WHERE THE BLACK TURNS TO GOLD
WHERE TIME NO LONGER HOLDS
REALITIES
ENTWINED

12.

WITHIN THE CAGE, A SMILE
RELIEF AT JOURNEY'S END
CHANCE TO COMPREHEND
AND TO
RECONCILE

13.

"LUCY TAYLOR, I AM HERE
I'M HERE TO TAKE YOU HOME
A WORLD FROZEN IN STONE
THEY AWAIT
THE SEER"

14.

"THE ONE WHO SAW THE TRUTH
THE GIRL THAT REMEMBERED
REALITIES EXTENDED
CHAPEL'S LEAKY
ROOF"

15.

"MANY SOULS HAVE BEEN LOST
DELETED FROM THE GAME
A CHANCE TO START AGAIN
TO COUNT THE
REAL COST"

16.

TO RESTART LIFE ON EARTH
FOR CLOCKS TO TICK THEIR TOCK
TO FREE THE CHRONOLOCK
REVELATION
REVERSED

17.

ON APOPHENIA NOW
WE MUST PLOT OUR RETURN
WE HAVE SO MUCH TO LEARN
WEIGH UP WHAT
IS FOUND

18.

OUR STEPS MUST NUMBER EIGHT
WE COUNT OUR INNER GROWTH
AND PLEDGE A SACRED OATH
REVERSE OUR PLANET'S FATE

19.

THE DAMAGE HAS BEEN DONE
BUT OUR TOOL IS ALL OF TIME
BREAK BREAD AND DRINK THE WINE
MAKE THE PAST
UNDONE

20.

HERE ON APOPHENIA
WE TICK A BETTER TOCK
A NEW HUMAN EPOCH
ANTHROPOCENE, YEAH

21.

THIS SIMULATION ENDS
WHEN ELON CAN'T CONTROL
THE POWER OF THE SOUL
YOU ARE
ALREADY DEAD

22.

EIGHT STAGES OF REBIRTH
EIGHT CIRCUITS TO COMPLETE
ANAMNESIS RETREATS
RECONNECT
THE EARTH

23.

REMOVE OUR LATEST SIN

DELETE OUR DARKEST DANCE

EARN EARTH A SECOND CHANCE

AND SO IT

BEGINS

RITES

OF

PASS-AGE

1.

YOU ARE THE STUFF OF STARS

BRIGHT ILLUMINATION

INDRA'S NET EQUATION

YOU ARE NEAR

AND FAR

2.

YOU ARE THE UNIVERSE

YOU ARE THE CPU

ALL CONNECTED TO YOU

CIRCUITS NOW

REVERSED

3.

INCALCULABLE REALMS
INDIVISIBLE VOID
ALL DISTANCES DESTROYED
THE POWER
OVERWHELMS

4.

NEXT WE LEARN THE WISDOM
OF ALL THAT HAS BEEN SUNG
THE CONSCIOUSNESS THAT JUNG
DECLARED IN
'EVERYONE

5.

THE TRUTH OF EVOLUTION

YOU'RE WHAT HAS COME BEFORE

WE'RE ALL OF THEM BUT MORE

SUPER

INSTITUTION

6.

WITH CODED DNA

YOU ARE THE LIVING DEAD

THEIR THOUGHTS STAY IN YOUR HEAD

STILL WITH MUCH

TO SAY

7.

YOU ARE YOUR OWN DOMAIN

AWARE OF WHO YOU ARE

TELEPATHIC LODE STAR

GUIDES FROM WHERE

YOU CAME

8.

YOU ARE SELF-COMMUNION

YOU KNOW YOUR DESTINY

BUILD AND SHAPE REALITIES

FACILITATE

REUNION

9.

IT'S FAIR TO SAY WE'RE NOT

IN KANSAS ANYMORE

THE CAGE CREATES THE DOOR

TO WHAT WE

FORGOT

10.

YOU ARE YOUR BODY CIRCUIT

REWIRED FOR ECSTASY

REVERSE THE ENTROPY

BRING CHAOS

TO THE CLIFF

11.

YOU ARE YOUR OWN RAPTURE

SELF-GENERATED BLISS

EMBRACE THE AESTHETIC

OF WHAT COMES

AFTER

12.

HALFWAY HOME, A BOUNDARY

INNER AND OUTER SPACE

ENTACTOGENESIS

CAMARADERIE

13.

LIVE THROUGH THIS PETITE-MORT

YOU ARE THE FIRE'S GLOW

WITH FLAME, YOU SHOT ARROWS

'TIL YOU SHOT

NO MORE

14.

YOU ARE ALL EMPATHY

YOU HEAR OUR TALES OF WOE

AND WHILE WE ALL OFF-LOAD

YOU PROFFER

REMEDY

15.

YOU ARE THERE, ON THE MAP

THE WHOLE TERRITORY

SYMBOLIC HISTORY

ROUTES TO TAKE

YOU BACK

16.

YOU ARE THE WRITTEN WORD

YOU ARE THE POET'S QUILL

YOU ARE THE CAVE SYMBOLS

SPEAK ACROSS

THE YEARS

17.

YOU ARE CALCULATION

THE MEASURES AND THE RATES

YOU ARE THE TIME IT TAKES

FOR OSCILLATION

18.

YOU ARE THE ONES WE MEET

ALL TRUSTS AND SUSPICIONS

DOMINANCE/SUBMISSION

ELEMENTS

COMPETE

19.

YOU ARE SHELTER IN STORM

YOU ARE FOOD THAT FEEDS ME

GROWS MY BONES BENEATH ME

BLANKET IN

THE WARM

20.

YOU ARE THE HOUSE WE BUILT

ON STRONG FOUNDATION STONE

YOU ARE ONE VOICE ALONE

UNTIL SEED

IS SPILT

21.

FROM ALL WE ARE NOTHING

WE ARE TAKEN APART

ANOTHER CHANCE TO START

REDIRECT

DISCUSSION

22.

FROM THE GRAVE TO CRADLE

YOU'LL FIND YOURSELF REBORN

LIVE A NEW LIFE AGAIN

SECOND CHANCE

ENABLED

23.

YOUR JOURNEY'S AT AN END
THIS STORY MADE FOR YOU
AND I MUST ASSURE YOU
WE WILL MEET AGAIN

START

THE

CLOCK

1.

AS WE RETURN TO EARTH

WE ARRIVE IN THE PAST

TWENTY-THREE YEARS IN FACT

FOR LUCY'S

REBIRTH

2.

CAMACHO DRESSED IN BLACK

STARTS THE SEMINARY

YEARS BEFORE THE JOURNEY

THE BLACK ROOM

AND BACK

3.

SOMEHOW HE HAS RETAINED

A DISTANT MEMORY

OF DUSTY CALVARY

ASTRONAUT

REMAINS

4.

HIS LORD IS HIS SHEPHERD

HIS GOD IS HIS PASSION

TO FINDING HIS MISSION

SHE WHO

REMEMBERED

5.

CAMPBELL'S IN A LAB COAT

A LONG WAY FROM HER HOME

HOPING STUDIES WILL SHOW

DISCOVERIES

OF NOTE

6.

JET AND SKY ARE JUST TWINKLES

THEIR PARENTS BARELY TEENS

THEIR FATES YET TO BE SEEN

REALITY WILL

CRINKLE

7.

CAPTAIN CLARK LIES WITH EVE
THEIR LIVES AHEAD OF THEM
ALL THEIR LOVING CHILDREN
YET TO BE
CONCEIVED

8.

LIKE ANCESTORS BEFORE
HE LONGS TO STEER THE SHIP
HE LONGS TO TAKE THE TRIP
'TIL CURSE'S
NO MORE

9.

MAD ALAN SITS ALONE

HIS BOX OF TRICKS IS PRIMED

HIS MUSIC OUT OF TIME

YET TO FIND

A HOME

10.

YOUNG ANTON LIES IN COT

ENCHANTED BY THE CHIMES

THE MELODIES SUBLIME

WAITS FOR LIFE

TO START

11.

BOYD/ROSS WORKS THE SHIPYARDS
ALONG THE RIVER CLYDE
ONE DAY THEY'LL ROCKET RIDE
AND LIVE AMONG
THE STARS

12.

VINNIE SHUFFLES WITH NERVES
HIS FIRST DATE WITH MARIE
THEY WILL HAVE ETERNITY
LAST EMBRACE
PRESERVED

13.

JACK DAWES DRIVES A WHITE VAN

YEARS BEFORE THE BRICK DUST

YEARS BEFORE THE FURNESS

THAT BURNED UP

A BILLION

14.

THE ICE KREAM MEN WERE OUT

IN THEIR PINK ICE KREAM VAN

STILL WITH NO MASTER PLAN

'TIL OVER

AND OUT

15.

SILLY CROW WAS JUST AN EGG
AND YET TO SPREAD ITS WINGS
AND YET TO DO THE THINGS
THAT CHANGED ALL
DESTINIES

16.

SO LUCY WAKES REBORN
THE DAY SHE FOUND THE GLITCH
SHE'S YET TO THROW THE SWITCH
BRING ABOUT
NEW DAWNS

17.

WITH PARENTS TO THE PARK

SHE SITS ATOP A SLIDE

THEN REALITIES COLLIDE

CROW WITH FEATHERS DARK

18.

LUCY SEES CROW-FRIEND

OBSERVING FROM AFAR

HE SEES THAT HER FUTURE

LOOPS WITHOUT

AN END

19.

REVEALED IS LUCY'S CHORE
REMEMBER - TELL THEM ALL
EVOLVE, REVOLVE, RESOLVE
REPEAT FORE'ERMORE

20.

ON SWINGIN, SOHO STREETS
CHARLES WILL REBOOTED
AND SUPER-SHARP SUITED
AGAIN A
TIME THIEF

21.

ENDLESSLY DREAMS OF HER

A FOE OR MAYBE FRIEND

'TIL THEY MEET AGAIN

ON

APOPHENIA

22.

REAL ELON HAS A PLAN

QUIET REVOLUTION

A REVERT-SOLUTION

RESET THE

TIMELINE

23.

HE LOVES HER ENDEAVOUR

SHE HAS DONE THIS BEFORE

TWENTY-THREE TIMES OR MORE

KEEP LOOPING FOREVER

Aftermath

It is November 23rd 2017. Lucy Taylor's early night is wrecked by protesters chanting about mince pies. She gets up and starts baking.

It is 1st of Kislev 3790, Camacho rests at foot of Golgotha. He gazes up at the night sky. The universe gazes back.

It is 11 Tsuki 23-nichi 1927. Charles is making gifts for his local police as is the custom on Kinrō Kansha no Hi.

It is 23 Marraskuuta 1936. Professor Yrjö Väisälä is at the Turku Observatory. He finds a new object in the inner asteroid ring.

It takes exactly three years to orbit the sun. It is rich in iron (46%) and vanadium (23%). He names it 1454 Kalevala.

It is 23rd November 2023. Ralf is a lab assistant at Kline von Liebesfrequenz. He reviews the notes left by the previous shift.

Subject #128
Returned to ward.
Subject #129
Unsuitable. Discharged.
Subject #130
System failure. Disposal requested.
Subject #131
Test rescheduled.

Tonight will be another quiet shift for Ralf, but he has come prepared. He cracks the spine on a book he has found.

The book was left outside his dorm room last night. The cover intrigued him. A black isosceles triangle sits on a yellow background.

Inside the triangle there is a bright, white circle. For some unknown reason, the image resonates deeply with him. He begins to read.

Andy Gell is a fledgling writer from the South of the North of England.

After accidentally writing a play, a slavish dedication to acronyms and the number 23 has yielded a five book trilogy.

When pressed, he will always blame The Justified Ancients Of Mu Mu.

Follow his descent on Twitter as

@ReactionsTo2023

Illustration, lettering, design, and supplementary enchantments by

⚕ Peter Horneland, artist and vitki, born in Norway.

With gratitude to F23, S∴C∴, and The V. Rev. Roadkill Turnabouts XLIV.

Works can be found at

peterhorneland.com

Printed in Great Britain
by Amazon